Healing
the Hurt

Healing the Hurt

Help for Teenagers Whose Parents Are Divorced

Mildred Tickfer

BAKER BOOK HOUSE
Grand Rapids, Michigan 49506

Copyright 1984 by
Baker Book House Company

ISBN: 0-8010-8876-3

Printed in the United States of America

Scripture quotations identified LB are from The Living Bible © 1971 by Tyndale House Publishers.
Scripture quotations identified TEV are from The Bible in Today's English Version © 1966, 1971, 1976 by American Bible Society.

Contents

    Preface   7-8
1. Confusion: *I Don't Know What to Do*   9
2. Betrayal: *How Could They . . . ?*   21
3. Doubt and Fear: *Could They Stop Loving Me?*   31
4. Anger: *The Two-Edged Sword*   43
5. Grief: *Mourning the Loss*   51
6. In the Middle: *I Feel Like a Ping-Pong Ball*   63
7. Switching Roles: *I Don't Want to Be the Parent*   71
8. Jealousy: *Mom Has a New Boyfriend/Dad Has a New Wife*   79
9. Living: *Let's Get On with It*   87

    Suggested Reading   94

Preface

You are a teenager—and have just discovered that your parents are getting a divorce. Perhaps this is a shocking surprise. Or you may have been aware for some time that all was not well at home. Either way, the knowledge comes as painfully as if someone just punched you in the stomach. You feel betrayed, confused, hurt, guilty, scared, and angry.

This book will take a look at these feelings and others you may experience in the coming weeks and months. Although it will help you understand what is happening, this book is not a magic potion to make your emotions or this situation disappear. It is more like a rope thrown to a drowning person who can choose either to grab the lifeline and save himself or splash around in frantic panic and swallow the sea.

Some of the suggestions in this book will be like clothes you get for Christmas. They may not fit right now. Maybe you will grow into them; maybe they will never fit you. You can treat them as you do those Christmas clothes. Use what fits and pass the rest on to someone who needs it more than you do.

As a psychiatric nurse I have counseled several teens whose parents were divorced or divorcing. Frustrations, hurts, and concerns were accurately pinpointed with varying emotions. To gain additional insights, I've interviewed many teens who are or have coped with divorced parents. Names have been changed to insure privacy. But the situations are real and the scars are deep. Divorce is difficult for both teens and their parents. I've helped many teens to see there is hope for a brighter tomorrow. I pray that I can help you, too.

Mildred Tickfer

1

Confusion
I Don't Know What to Do

> The yelling and screaming was awful
> It woke me sometimes in the night.
> But I found it even more fright'ning
> When they were so coldly polite.

He sat in my kitchen, looking utterly miserable. Tears rolled down his cheeks. He stared at the floor. "I don't know what to do," he sobbed as he twisted his hands together. I just sat with him for a while, silently acknowledging his tears and misery. "I don't know what to do," he repeated.

"What do you want to do?" I asked.

"Get my parents back together." It was said with passion and urgency. For a week he had been living with the agony of knowing that his parents were separating. Divorce was not just a word anymore. It was a part of his nighttime terror and the cause of his daytime depression.

Can Anything Be Done?

If one or both of your parents has decided to get a divorce, there is probably nothing you can say or do to reverse that decision. Although they may change their mind(s), that is highly unlikely once this stage has been reached. It is important, however, for you to accept that it is *their* decision. Never forget that *you* are not responsible for the divorce. Nor do you have to feel guilty, embarrassed, or ashamed.

You will very likely feel sad, confused, and angry as you realize that their decision will have some far-reaching effects on your life. But you cannot make a decision about divorce for two other people. Even if the situation has been one of bickering and fighting for a long time—even if you have secretly wished that one or the other of your parents would leave, or even if you said that out loud—it is still their decision to make.

You cannot know what is best for someone else. Right now you probably cannot even guess what is best for you. But, right or wrong, the decision is made, and you cannot change it, nor should you feel any responsibility for doing so.

Much of your confusion may come from the fact that you love both your parents very much. Remember that it is their divorce from each other, not from you. Even though they choose to separate, they will both always be your parents. You may have to choose which one you will live with or spend more time with, but you do not have to choose which one you will love.

One of your parents may have already left and is probably not coming back. Even though your head knows that your parent's leaving had nothing to do with you, in your heart you feel deserted and miserable. Although the anger and the leaving have to do with two married adults, the fact is that you have been left also. It is natural to feel abandoned.

Keep On Loving and Communicating

Try to keep the lines of communication open with both parents as much as possible. This will become increasingly difficult if one parent is not living with you anymore.

Your parents need to know that you still love them. They need to be assured of this by you just as badly as you need to hear it from them. If you know where the absent parent is, a regular postcard or letter in the mail might be appropriate. For the live-in parent, a note slipped in a lunch box or left on a pillow will be a way you can say, "I love you and I still need you." See how creative you can be.

Remember that you are not the only one hurting right now; a parent whose spouse is leaving or has already done so is usually feeling very hurt and unlovable. It is extremely difficult for most people to see beyond their own hurts. So do not be surprised if your once-sensitive parent suddenly seems blind to your emotional needs.

What If My Parents Don't Care About Me?

Of course, there are some parents who are so wrapped up in their own concerns that they truly do not care if their teenagers are hurting. Though rare, this may be your situation. You may feel that your parents do not care anything about you as a person. This is a big challenge for a teen, or even for a mature adult. The natural reaction is: "If my own parent doesn't love me, I must be a pretty awful person." And if all of the anger you might justifiably direct toward your deserting parent is turned inward, you can become an emotional wreck.

Greg

When Greg was fifteen his father left suddenly. There was no further communication. There was no support money and no evidence that his father still existed. But Greg could not escape the feeling that this meant he was a rotten kid. His behavior deteriorated rapidly. He regressed to wetting the bed at night.

Janyce

Although actually relieved when her father left, Janyce felt guilty, too. "I sort of felt like I was to blame. During the last year that my parents were together, my dad and I got into a lot of fights over stupid things. He'd always say that he would stay until I turned eighteen. But that summer he said, 'I can't take it,' and he left."

She interpreted that to mean that her dad could not stand *her*. Janyce continued, "Well, he was always being really mean to me and telling me that he didn't love me and everything. And so I thought I must be to blame."

Perhaps you feel guilty. You see your parents as bigger and older, and naturally they are wiser (you think). So if someone got this family in a mess it must be "young, dumb, little" you. This is one of the first myths you need to dump in the garbage can.

Marie

I asked Marie what was most difficult for her. She replied, "Responsibility was one. I guess it really bothered me to see my mother so distressed. She had rarely gotten so upset before. My father was never a strong person. And all of a sudden I was facing two "not strong" people. After I had counted on her for so many things for so long, I now saw her falling apart on me. She went to work every day, and she was very responsible at work. But when she came home she very much needed to be comforted, which I understand. But I needed to be comforted, too, and she didn't have the energy to give me that right then."

Bert

Explained Bert: "When my folks were breaking up I knew Dad didn't want any of us kids. I felt like it was all my fault. Even though I had seen him with that other lady, I thought that if I had told Dad 'Stop!' right then, maybe he would have stopped right then. Or, if I had told Mom early enough, or if I could have talked to that other guy. . . . I don't know if it would have done any good. In fact, I doubt that it would have. We had quite a few incidents of my dad just coming right out and saying he didn't want us."

Andy

When his parents split, Andy was away at college. He said, "I think one of the most important things for me to realize was that I was not responsible for what happened. And in the first couple of months I did feel that way. I played with thoughts of dropping out of school. My mother was in a tight financial situation. The alimony had not been settled, and she had to move out of her house because the house was to be sold and the capital split. But my parents talked to me about that. Both my parents said to me, 'It's not your responsibility. Don't take it as your responsibility.' I think it was very good of them to say that to me because that way my feeling of guilt lasted only a couple of months.

"A bigger thing on my mind has been: What caused it to happen? And I wasn't even looking for anyone to blame. Again, both of my parents said, 'We're both at fault. There are problems at both ends, and there are problems that started right after we got married.'"

Andy was fortunate that his parents were so open with him. Many parents figure that since the divorce is between them, their kids need not know what is going on. Sometimes they think their children are too young to understand. In other cases, the parents' own disappointment and pain make it difficult to discuss the situation with them.

However, as one teen said, "Kids need to know a little bit about what's going on. It's awful not knowing. Even if the situation changes from day to day, kids should be kept informed."

Lori

"Unfortunately, at thirteen I was a little too smart for my

britches," Lori admitted. "I got hold of a lot of information indirectly that I shouldn't have. My dad had been having an affair and, through a remarriage, there were other children that were going to become his within a year. Things like that really crushed me. This was information I should have received from my father."

If You Need Information, Try Asking!

If your parents are not talking to you about what is going on, and you feel you need more answers, ask. Explain to them that it will help you to make sense out of the situation only if you have some information and that you prefer to get it from them and not have to resort to town gossip.

Keep in mind that there are some details that should remain private. Not everything that happens between a man and woman should become public information, even to their children. So don't press for the intimate details. But it is realistic to ask to be kept informed of what is happening.

Here are some valid questions you may ask: What legal suit is being brought? By whom? Is there a countersuit? Are court dates set? Will you be expected to make an appearance in court? When will the divorce be final? Who will have custody? Where will you live? These are questions to which you are entitled to have answers. Since this information may change, ask for updates if they are not volunteered.

Penny

For Penny, it has been like living inside of a raging thunderstorm that never moves on. Her parents' divorce was final when she was only six years old. Her all-consuming question was, "Why?" She reports, "As I was growing up, it was really hard because other kids didn't understand it. So I got picked on quite often. It hurt a lot. And it still does, thirteen years later.

They're still going through court procedures and all kinds of things. It's just a very unsettling thing. I've never seen two people hate each other so much."

For most teens, the pain does not continue to be so acute for so long. Few parents are still fighting in court thirteen years after the original divorce decree is final. Many divorced parents manage to be civil and some are even friendly with each other after the smoke of a fiery divorce has cleared.

Why Do Parents Divorce, Anyway?

Parents seek a divorce for a wide variety of reasons. Sometimes, one parent feels the other one can no longer be trusted. He or she may or may not have reasons to feel that way. In most cases, communication has completely broken down and the partners are unable to share at a feeling level. When a couple is seeking a divorce, there is no longer a mutual commitment to the continued growth of the other person or to the marriage itself. Divorcing persons tend to get caught up in the what-is-right-for-me mentality, but they generally believe it is better for the children not to be subjected to their parents' continual bickering and fighting. Very often one parent is devastated because the other has left them for someone else. Whatever the situation at your house, be assured it is not happening because of you.

Jim

For Jim, the confusion is in the fact that there never was any fighting. His dad just decided that he did not want to be married anymore, so he moved away. But he missed Jim and his brother so much that after a couple of years he moved back into the same community. Now Jim spends every weekend with his dad and during the week lives with his mother. His parents are pleasant to each other. If Jim messes up at school, they both come to the teacher conferences. Neither parent has remarried. The big question for Jim is, "If Mom and Dad are so friendly with each other and so concerned about me, why don't they get married again so we can get back to being one big happy family?" And his mom says, "I can't help you understand it, Jim. I don't really understand it myself."

Does God Really Care?

Where is God in all of this? Does He know about your pain? Does He care? The image of a loving Heavenly Father may have little meaning for someone whose earthly parents cannot keep it together. It is difficult enough to imagine an unseen being out there somewhere who loves you. And what is love, anyway? Your parents used to love each other, but that seems to have come to a screeching halt. If their love was so temporary, who needs it? Perhaps you even think, "God was some kind of a Father, too—letting His own son die for other people's mistakes. I'm not ready to buy into that right now. . . ."

If you have had thoughts like these, it is not surprising. You are in a very hard place, and people in tough situations often react by being angry at God. Some, unfortunately, even turn away from Him completely.

Let's think about this carefully. When God created this world He planned it to be a happy place. He provided a beautiful garden setting for Adam and Eve, with plenty of vegetation and animals for food and their other needs. His plan for the human family was one man, one woman, and their children.

Since God wanted Adam and Eve to be responsible for taking care of both the Garden of Eden and their family, He gave them the right to make choices. Although this Bible story is familiar to most of us, maybe you would like to read it again in Genesis, chapters 1 and 2.

Men and women have been making poor choices ever since Adam and Eve made their blooper in the Garden of Eden. Some of the poor choices have had disastrous results. These mistakes have been disappointing for the Lord. In fact, on one occasion He went so far as to say, "I'm so sick of all this mess that I'm going to destroy everyone but the one man who still loves Me and is making good choices." This is a familiar Bible story, too. You can read it in Genesis, chapters 6 and 7.

Did you notice that when God started over with Noah, His plan for the family was still the same? One man, one woman, and their children. The total wipe-out was pretty devastating punishment for mankind's bad choices, and God made a promise that He would never do that again. Of course, He did not promise there would be no more punishment, just no more total destruction by flood.

In the original agreement, God said that men and women must obey His commandments or they would have to suffer the consequences. God gave mankind a set of laws to live by, and when any of those laws was broken the result would be pain and punishment. God's original covenant allowed for people to receive forgiveness by making sacrifices and offerings.

But people continued to mess up, and God continued to discipline them to demonstrate His concern for them. "I love you, My children. I want you to make good choices. When you make bad choices there will be pain, suffering, and sometimes punishment."

Unfortunately, when one or two persons make a wrong choice that suffering may include a lot of innocent people. Whole nations have been caught up in wars as a result of a bad decision by a few people. But God has said, "I will send My own son as an example of real love. He will show my people how much I love them. He will become the sacrifice for all the sins of all the world."

Look at the way God chose to do it. It was back to His original plan for families—one man, one woman, and (slight variation, here) God's own son. But God put such a high value on family that He placed even His own son, Jesus, in a home with a mother and a father. He did not have to do it that way. Since Joseph was not really Jesus' biological father, God could have left Joseph out altogether. This story can be read in Luke, chapters 1 and 2.

What does all this have to do with you? How does it relate to what is happening at your house? God's plan for the family seems to be falling apart in your home (and others). We could dump it all back on God by saying, "He should never have given man a choice." If you think about that one long enough, I bet you will not be real crazy about the alternative, either. The point is, if we start blaming God for our troubles instead of turning to Him for help, we shut Him out. We stop listening to His plans, and we make wrong choices ourselves. To say, "I don't need God. He is letting me down; if God loved me, this wouldn't be happening," is blaming God because someone else made some wrong choices.

Right now, the thing for you to do is to look at your relationship with Jesus. Although you are not responsible for the divorce, you may have made some poor choices as far as your relationship with the Lord is concerned. Have you been blaming Him for what is happening to you?

Even if you have done and said some things for which you are sorry, you do not have to do any sacrificing to pay for your mistakes. God did that already, remember? He sacrificed His son. We have only to ask for and accept His gift of forgiveness, and with that we receive some other very special blessings. Isn't it about time something good was coming your way? Here it is from The Living Bible. You may also want to read it in some other version:

> So now, since we have been made right in God's sight by faith in his promises, we can have real peace with him because of what Jesus Christ our Lord has done for us.
> For because of our faith, he had brought us into this place of highest privilege where we now stand, and we confidently and joyfully look forward to actually becoming all that God has had in mind for us to be,

We can rejoice, too, when we run into problems and trials for we know that they are good for us—they help us learn to be patient.

And patience develops strength of character in us and helps us trust God more each time we use it until finally our hope and faith are strong and steady.

Romans 5:1–4 LB

Janyce

Right about now I am sure you figure you could have done without this character-building experience! I asked Janyce what had helped her the most to get through her experience.

"My youth group, Campus Life, and the leaders there. They talked to me and read to me from the Bible. Spiritually, I've grown. I'm stronger now than I've ever been."

When I asked Janyce what she would like to tell other teenagers who are in this situation, she said, "Find someone you can talk to and try to talk to your parents, too. See what's really bothering them. Why they're divorcing. Be up front. Be direct. And pray a lot."

2

BETRAYAL
How Could They . . . ?

> Happiness is a bluebird
> That cannot be caged.
> Last week my family
> Bought a crippled crow.

All your life you have been brought up to believe that some behaviors are wrong and others right. The reasons given for certain things being wrong are often biblical. Sometimes the standards are based on specific church rules or on society's laws or on generally accepted behavior patterns in the community. Both religious and governmental laws form the foundation of acceptable moral standards. But for most of us, what makes something "wrong" is to have our parents say it is wrong.

In the next few years, you will be thinking about these right-and-wrong issues more than at any time in your whole lifetime. You will be formulating, revising, and establishing your own code of moral behavior. You might decide that some behaviors your parents said were wrong are not so wrong. Or you might decide that some of the standards your parents found acceptable are not right for you.

What you were not prepared for was to see your parents doing some of the very things they have brought you up to believe were wrong. This contributes to your feeling of confusion and adds a sense of betrayal.

How Do We Know What Is Right?

The Ten Commandments of the Old Testament (see Exodus 20:1–17) and the two New Testament statements (see Mark 12:29–31) that summarize the Law, and are quoted by Jesus, are the primary standards of right and wrong. God's standards never change. They are absolutes against which we measure all else. What changes are people's interpretations of those standards.

Old Testament Laws

1. I am the Lord your God. Put no other gods before Me.
2. Do not worship images or idols.
3. Do not use the name of the Lord your God carelessly.
4. Observe the Sabbath Day and keep it holy.
5. Show respect to your father and mother.
6. Do not kill.
7. Do not commit adultery.
8. Do not steal.
9. Do not bear false witness against your neighbor.
10. Do not desire anything that is your neighbor's.

New Testament Commandments

1. Love the Lord your God with all your heart, soul, and strength. This is the first and great commandment. The second is very much like it.
2. Love your neighbor the way you love yourself.

It's Hard to Accept Your Parent's Mistakes

Maybe you are struggling to find an interpretation that will convince you that what one or both of your parents is doing is right. It is hard for teenagers who have had a strong relationship with their parents to accept that Mom and Dad can and often do make mistakes. It is especially difficult to believe that parents would deliberately do something wrong. Children want their parents to be perfect. It is embarrassing and therefore difficult for teenagers to accept their parents' imperfections.

Since you may have identified strongly with your parents—or one of them—if they made a mistake, somehow you feel as if it was your mistake, too. That is why teenagers feel ashamed or embarrassed when they recognize that their parents are wrong in a particular situation. But that is one aspect of being part of a family.

Parents feel that way about their children, too. Remember when you were little and were visiting friends or relatives? If you did something naughty, your parents apologized for your behavior. They acted as if it were their fault, although this made you feel like you had really let them down.

Now the shoe is on the other foot, and you are the one who is really feeling let down. You are caught in the middle. Either what they said was wrong is not wrong anymore, or what they are doing is actually wrong. It doesn't feel very good either way.

How Do You Handle Your Parents' Mistakes?

You may have already begun to sort out your values, ideals, and principles. One of the ways you do this is by bouncing them off your parents' goals, values, and principles. And just when you thought you had things all figured out, you saw them disintegrating right before your eyes. Now you are not sure what is right anymore.

This is where some kids get really mixed up and start to mess up. They get into drugs, alcohol, and other people's fast cars. Although this appears to ease the pain or replaces disappointment with a heady excitement, it does nothing about the original problem. Such short-term relief only postpones the time when it must be dealt with on a constructive level.

The relief that can be found in drugs, alcohol, and other sensation-deadening measures is only temporary. Then you need more to feel better. And pretty soon you are caught in a whirlpool that threatens to suck you under.

The standards remain. If turning left on Pleasant Street was the wrong way for you to get to Utopia last month, it is still the wrong direction for you—even if you just saw Mom or Dad go that way.

Pedestals Are Precarious

All fathers and mothers fall from their pedestals sooner or later. No one is perfect. Eventually, anyone who is honest must admit that no human being, including Dad or Mom, will ever in this life sprout wings or wear halos. Actually, pedestals are uncomfortable, and maybe the most unfair thing we do to anyone is put them up there. A person on a pedestal can hardly make a move without tipping over that perch and falling.

Lori

Lori said, "My dad fell off his pedestal—and hard! Unfortunately, in my eyes, he hasn't been able to get back up on it."

It does sound as if Lori's dad took a bad fall, though. Does that mean she stops loving him? No, probably not, although she has had her illusions of his perfection shattered. Now she knows he is human and very imperfect, as are all humans. Father and daughter might be able to rebuild their relationship if she is willing to forgive him.

You may be saying, as one young girl did, "My parents didn't just make a mistake. It wasn't just a little slip-up. It was a wrong act. My parents knew it was wrong. It was wrong according to all of the standards I've been brought up to believe. How could they do that? That's defiance of the law. It's like deliberately driving through a red light."

Not only are you embarrassed by your parents' shortcomings; you are disappointed and confused. This is the essence of betrayal—someone you trusted is doing what he or she told you was wrong.

If you are one of the many teens who have heard more arguments between your parents than you care to count, you are probably well aware that neither one of them is perfect. Parents can and do make mistakes. Some of them could be very serious.

Bert

Here is a part of a conversation I had with Bert, who observed, "You always think your dad's the greatest, you know."

I answered, "It had to be terribly disappointing to discover your dad was . . ."

Bert broke in, "Doing that! Yeah! I figure people make mistakes, but I think he made quite a few of them."

Lori

"I guess the thing I had to work through—and which I did in a very poor way—was whose fault it was," said Lori. "I guess I believed that divorce was wrong. You hear that certain things are right and certain things are wrong. And at that time in my moral development, divorce was wrong. I didn't understand why it had to happen. And my dad was the 'bad guy' for me because he was the one who took off and left a sick wife and four children. It was a difficult scene. So I faced the ongoing process of trying to figure out in my head that the wrong was done and how I fit into it."

Andy

Finding answers takes time. As Andy said, "For me, my parents were always a base to bounce things off, and I had been introduced to different ways of thinking. And my mother is someone who is a devil's advocate continually. If you came up with one statement, she'd come up with a counterexample. But if you came up with a counterstatement, she'd come up with a counter to that. So she was always challenging me in that respect. And I always admired that. It tempered me. I don't think I could ever be a radical anymore. She has taught me that there are always two sides and that there's likely a gray area on most issues. She made me feel that there's not just black and white. I'm not convinced that's true across the board, so I'm still trying to figure things out myself. Also, I've looked to other people, people in my church and friends at college."

Shirley

Part of the feelings of betrayal for Shirley came after her mother remarried. For her mom the initial pain of the separation and divorce was over, and Shirley admitted that her mother "was very happy with her new husband." Mom was upset with Shirley, however, because she still wanted to see her father and spend time with him. Both Mom and her new husband said cruel, cutting things about her dad, and Shirley felt that this was "extremely unfair. After all, he is still my father." And even though Shirley did not always approve of his lifestyle, she still felt strong affection for him.

Patti

While still an infant, Patti was adopted into what appeared to be a stable, loving Christian home. But something went wrong somewhere along the line, and her parents separated and later divorced. Patti was angry: "If they couldn't stay together, why did they adopt me? It's a broken promise. And it hurts."

Missy

An especially strong feeling of betrayal was felt by Missy. Her father was a minister. Missy knew that "he and Mom were not getting along exactly well, but I was not prepared for what happened." He left their family and started living with the choir director, who also left her family.

For Missy there was more than the loss of father and family. There was the painful embarrassment of her dad's having made a grave error of judgment. "It was awful," she said, "to see my father chastized by the church and asked to resign from the pastorate."

After the Trauma, Comes Healing

None of us gets through this life without making mistakes, some of which are bigger than others. Some errors are as visible as a scab on the end of your nose. Others may prove to be embarrassing to you, but not too many other people ever know about them. A divorce is like that scab on the end of your nose. Everybody seems to know about it. But, as with all scabs, eventually there is healing and the scab disappears. If the wound is deep, there may be a scar. But even scars fade in time.

Don't Be Too Judgmental

Realistically, it is very difficult for us to be loving and accepting of someone who is doing something we believe to be wrong. It may help to remember that in God's final judgment there will be a much broader base of knowledge and understanding than we can possibly have.

Perhaps we should leave the judging to God and apply ourselves to the loving. The highest form of loving is unconditional. This means that we love someone not because of what they do or say. We love them just for being who they are. Is it right—or even possible—for you to love each of your parents, even while despising their behavior? The Bible says: "Do not judge others, so that God will not judge you, for God will judge you in the same way you judge others, and he will apply to you the same rules you apply to others" (Matthew 7:1–2, TEV).

Chris

"I'm all for forgiveness," said Chris. "I'm all for loving them with all my heart, but sometimes I have a real hard time even liking my parents. They did botch things up, and they did it on a grand scale! And forgiving them? How do you know if you've forgiven somebody? I can say to you, 'You just hit me. I forgive you.' But you never forget the initial act."

Can You Forgive If You Can't Forget?

It is not all-important for us to forget the shortcomings of others. In fact, remembering may serve to remind us not to make the same mistakes. Jesus commanded us to forgive seventy times seven times, which has been interpreted to mean an infinite number of times. But Jesus did not ask us to forget even once.

In I Corinthians 13:5, we read that love "is not rude, it is not self-seeking, it is not easily angered, it keeps no record of wrongs" (LB).

Forgiving does not make a wrong act right. It does not change the fact that it happened. We do not have to stick our heads ostrichlike in the sand and pretend that everything is okay. Everything is not okay. But you must be ready to love and forgive, as God the Father forgives your own errors.

It is important to recognize that the purpose of your parents' divorce was not to cause you pain. If there was wrong action on the part of one or both of your parents prior to the divorce, that was not done to hurt you either.

Look at the reasons behind your parents' behavior. Even if you consider it to be wrong, as an emerging adult, you can try to comprehend some of the whys. If you can begin to understand just a little, you are on the way to forgiving. This does not mean you have to condone the errors. Wrong is still wrong. You only have to try to understand.

Recognizing and acknowledging that a parent has made a mistake does not give you a license to stop loving or supporting him or her. If parents reacted that way toward the mistakes of their children, most of us would have been homeless at a very tender age. Part of loving is accepting that other person, faults included. Don't forget:

> Be always humble, gentle, and patient. Show your love by being tolerant with one another.
>
> Ephesians 4:2, TEV
>
> You are the people of God; he loved you and chose you for his own. So then, you must clothe yourselves with compassion, kindness, humility, gentleness, and patience. Be tolerant with one another and forgive one another whenever any of you has a complaint against someone else. You must forgive one another just as the Lord has forgiven you. And to all these qualities add love, which binds all things together in perfect unity.
>
> Colossians 3:12–14, TEV

3

Doubt and Fear
Could They Stop Loving Me?

> In the dark of night
> My fears are tight
> They surround me in my bed.
> In the daytime light
> I feel alright
> Except for doubts that fill my head.

One of the most frightening fears that might be hanging around the outer edges of your mind—you don't want to think about it but it won't go away—is: "If Mom and Dad could stop loving each other, could they stop loving me, too?"

The Absent Parent

That scary thought is one that could have a base in reality. When one parent moves out of the house and you do not see or hear from the absent one very often (or not at all), this fear grows even larger. Support payments that are late or fail to come at all may seem to be further proof that this parent no longer loves you.

In some families, this may actually be the case. A parent may be so caught up in caring only for self that there will be no room left to love others, even his or her children.

Mary Lou

"When I heard my dad leave," said Mary Lou, "I was afraid I'd never see him again. He sounded so angry. When he said he was never coming back, I figured that was it. He was gone for good."

In other families the absent parent is caught up in fighting with the custodial parent. He or she does not recognize that such acts of hostility toward a former spouse as late or insufficient support payments are taken personally by the children. In these households the angry feelings between the parents act like a smoke screen, keeping the parents from seeing that the children are experiencing fear of loss of love and feelings of abandonment. A few clear statements from you—in person or by mail—may help to blow the smog away. You might try something like, "When I don't hear from you for such a long time and I don't know where you are, I think you don't really love me anymore." Or, "When the support payment is late I feel as if I'm just a bother to you and you'd rather not have anything to do with me."

The Rejecting Parent

Another fear confronting some teenagers is: "What if the parent I want to live with doesn't choose to have me?" Again this is a realistic fear that must be faced.

Perhaps you have not clearly expressed your wishes to your parents, or it may be that it is not physically feasible because of parental illness. Or it may be financially impossible for you to live with the parent of your choice.

If your chosen parent has a new romantic interest, there may be no room in the honeymoon cottage or apartment for an offspring from a former alliance. That realization may shock like a glass of cold water thrown in your face, but you do not have to drown in it and feel as though you are an unwanted "leftover." Because your parent has other interests right now, you do not have to consider your relationship permanently severed. Nor should you interpret this to mean that something is wrong with you as a person.

It can be a big help to remember all of the good things your parents and others have said about you. Those worthwhile qualities have not changed. You are still a good, likeable person. It is okay to feel good about yourself, even when it seems as though your whole world is coming apart.

The Fear of Physical Abuse

Some kids have another fear. This is that one parent may physically hurt either him/herself or the other parent.

Bert

"We were supposed to go up North hunting," recalls Bert. "All of a sudden my mom and dad just started fighting and then they went downstairs and were fighting, and he gets carried away and says, 'Well, I just don't want you guys anymore.'

"He walks out the door. I say, 'See you later.' And I was crying and all upset. And he goes, 'No, you won't.' And I'll never forget that."

I asked Bert, "Did you ever have the feeling that he meant 'I won't be around because I'll do something to myself'?"

"That's what I thought. I had collected all the guns because we were going rabbit hunting, but he took them."

This was an extremely frightening experience for Bert. And he felt totally helpless to intervene.

Debby

"My mom became a pretty heavy drinker," Debby told me. "I was afraid she'd get in serious trouble and even get arrested. I knew she was really, really sick but she wouldn't let anybody help her."

If you have overheard threats or have other reasons to believe that someone in your family may be in danger or even in serious trouble, run—do not walk—to the nearest understanding adult you know. This is not a time to think about embarrassing either parent or the family name. Someone's life may be in danger. Do not attempt to intervene yourself. You are too involved emotionally and relationally to be effective in this situation.

Tell the person in whom you choose to confide what you fear and the grounds for those fears. You may wish to go to a pastor or other spiritual leader, your family doctor, a trusted school counselor, the parent of a close friend, or directly to a law enforcement or social agency. Another member of the family is usually not a good choice, since he or she is apt to react more emotionally than rationally. Do not be afraid to acknowledge your feelings. Admit, "I am frightened."

Fear of Financial Hardship

A fear that many teenagers suffer is based on financial concerns. If the family has been just getting by, or the income and assets are barely comfortably supporting one household, how will it survive supporting two? The legal fees and other expenses of separation can add up to astronomical figures. Although it is not your responsibility to raise the money to pay for your parents' divorce, the outcome may affect your lifestyle. You may no longer be able to afford some of the niceties of life that you have enjoyed in the past.

Eating out, bowling, pizza with the gang, and trips to the amusement park may have to be cut back sharply. You may even need to find a part-time job to pay for some of the necessities that were always provided in the past. Shampoo, toothpaste, deodorant, and other personal items may well become your responsibility.

You can react to this in one of two ways. You may sulk and rebel and fuss about life not being fair. Or you can snap to and assume your responsibility without grumbling. If it is impossible for you to find a part-time job or work one into an already busy schedule, you can still contribute to the family economy program. Carefully help manage your resources and those of the family. Turn off lights when you are not in a room. To trim the water bill, shorten the time you spend in the shower. Shop the local garage sales for your casual clothes. This is an opportunity to develop some fiscal management skills that will prove valuable all your life. You can either rise to the challenge—or let your fear of the financial future turn you into a whining infant.

The Fear of Peer Rejection

There is a feeling of isolation that comes from thinking that none of your crowd knows what it feels like when parents divorce. Check around. Probably close to half of your friends have been in this same situation. Some of them have been there more than once.

Some kids are afraid that once everyone knows about their parents' divorce, no one will like them or want them around anymore. Having your family disintegrate is in some ways like having your tonsils removed. Before, you had times when you did not feel well. When you wanted to do something special you could not participate in the fun, because you had a sore throat. You were very unhappy because you had this problem.

Then, when the doctor said that you were going to have a tonsillectomy, you thought, "Good! At least, I won't have any more sore throats." But, even so, you got worried because this was a new and scary experience. And things would be happening to you over which you would have no control. Although you wished the operation was not necessary, you were not crazy about the alternative, either.

Then came the surgery. You experienced pain, perhaps the worst sore throat you ever had. For a while people made a fuss over you and took care of you while you were hurting. Pretty soon, however, they forgot and went back to treating you normally. But you still hurt some. You did not even want to do some of the things you used to really enjoy, like eating popcorn and yelling at football games.

But, gradually, healing took place. In fact, there is no visible scar. No one even knows you have had your tonsils out unless you tell them. And the more time that goes by, the less people care. They are interested only in the total you. Who you are and what you like to do is more important than whether or not you have tonsils—or divorced parents.

Dealing with an Incompetent Parent

Mary

No longer did Mary's mother feel she could cope with the incompetence of Mary's father, who had been unstable for years. Mary said, "I wondered what my responsibilities were going to be toward my father, 'cause all of a sudden I realized my mother wasn't going to assume any responsibility for him. My brother had already graduated from college and was married and was off in California. So I thought, 'Guess who gets to take care of the program now.' Right then my father was insisting that he be admitted into a hospital. So we had him in a veterans' hospital for nine months. It was kind of hard because I had to go back to college. But then I always had to be in contact with the social worker because there was placement and review and all sorts of stuff. Then we found this group home for him and he really liked it. So it took a great load off my mind that there was such a thing. What does an eighteen- or nineteen-year-old know about group homes?

"There were a lot of legal matters to handle, including the money and the divorce settlement. And my father was incapable of handling his own funds. I was away at college and couldn't give him fifty dollars a week, so we had to set up a conservatorship. There had to be someone there to take care of his finances and other immediate needs. All of that was new and strange to me, and I had to depend on a lot of people. And I had to trust that they were telling me the truth, because I didn't know about such matters."

Mary represents a vast number of kids whose parents' divorce results from the mental illness of one parent. Perhaps the disturbance was present for a long time, and the other parent just could not cope any longer, as in Mary's situation. Or perhaps the ill parent fell apart suddenly. Either way, a fear wells up in adolescents that they, too, might develop mental illness. If the parent is hospitalized and the diagnosis indicates a chronic condition, it becomes even more frightening. And it helps little to have the other parent referring to the ill partner as "crazy."

A fear like this is particularly devastating if you cannot talk about it with someone. A good safe place to start is with a school counselor or your family doctor. Or a mental health clinic in your community may be able to help you. A fear as big as this one will be resolved most effectively by talking to a mental health professional. This may be a psychiatrist, psychologist, psychiatric nurse, social worker, or a pastor who has had special training in counseling. It will be reassuring to talk to someone who can understand and explain the dynamics of your parent's illness. When you understand it better, it will be less frightening for you. Parents who are mentally unstable especially need your support and love. Separation from them is a painful process.

There are many professional specialists in the field of mental-health care. An understanding of their training, background, and orientation may help you in dealing with a mentally ill parent:

Psychiatrist: A medical doctor who has had specialized training in the medical study, diagnosis, treatment, and prevention of mental illness. May prescribe medications.

Psychologist: A person trained to perform psychological testing, therapy, and/or research. A psychologist with a Ph.D. also will have the title of "doctor," although his or her training is not in medicine.

Psychiatric Nurse: A registered nurse qualified by education and/or experience to help in the care of patients having emotional disorders. He or she may work in conjunction with other mental-health workers or may have an independent practice.

Psychiatric Social Worker: A person trained in the adaptation and application of mental hygiene and social psychiatry to casework practice. Usually concerned with the social case study of persons whose personal and social maladjustments are primarily due to mental health problems. May work closely with other family members.

Bob

It did not take long for Bob to figure out that his mom was unstable emotionally. He could never believe her promises. He made the conscious decision, however, to make plans with his mother and even risk disappointment rather than not make any plans at all. And when the plans did not materialize, he usually could recognize that the weakness was his mother's.

Growth Means Becoming More Independent

Some of the fears teenagers have when their parents are divorcing revolve around a growth process shared by all adolescents—to begin separating from one's parents. You should want to become more independent, make more decisions for yourself, and try your freedom wings. But when the wings do not always work right and you come crashing down, you like to be able to come back home and find it a safe place to mend that broken wing.

A family whose structure is becoming unglued is not a secure nest for wing mending, because parents who are hurting themselves may be insensitive to your pain. They may yell at you to take your crummy injured wings off the coffee table! So, you ask, "Where is it safe?" The feelings of insecurity are enough to make some kids pack their broken wings in styrofoam and hide them in the back of the closet, forgetting that they ever wanted to fly.

Regardless of what is happening with Mom and Dad, you do not have to give up your dreams of free flight. You may need to look around for another adult who is a more likely flight instructor. It might be a teacher, an aunt or uncle, a grandparent, or just a good friend. It should be someone who genuinely likes you and who is not directly involved in an adult version of wing failure, one who has genuine, worthwhile qualities admired by you and the community at large.

Handling Adolescent Self-Consciousness

One of the normal problems which many adolescents have at this stage of life is being very self-conscious about the rapid physical and emotional changes they are experiencing. You have no doubt shared some of your confusing feelings about them with your teenage friends.

If self-consciousness is flowing in your veins, it may take real courage to dare to believe that an adult who is not your parent could genuinely like you. This is particularly difficult if you are feeling unloved by your own parent(s). I challenge you to grab your courage and test it out. But don't defeat yourself before you begin. Look around and choose wisely that person who best fits some worthy criteria. Then talk about your thoughts, dreams, even your doubts, with him or her. The positive feedback will help.

The next step is important, too. Believe in your own worth. Consider your assets, your positive qualities, your special aptitudes. You have something to offer in any relationship.

Always remember that although your folks are divorcing—and one parent is no longer a part of the home scene—it does not necessarily mean that you were part of the reason the absent parent sought escape.

Seek Divine Guidance and Strength

One of the fears some kids have stems from an overwhelming, almost smothering sensation. "What will happen to me? How will I get through this?" Don't panic! Seek out that person who has been most helpful to you in sorting your deepest feelings and spiritual beliefs. This may be your pastor, youth-group advisor, or a teacher. Reexamine your Christian faith and take hold of this promise:

> . . . .But God keeps his promise, and he will not allow you to be tested beyond your power to remain firm; at the time you are put to the test, he will give you the strength to endure it, and so provide you with a way out.
>
> 1 Corinthians 10:13, TEV

When all of these fears are swarming around you like an army of enemies, perhaps you can learn to say as David did:

> The Lord is my light and my salvation; I will fear no one.
> The Lord protects me from all danger; I will never be afraid.
> When evil men attack me and try to kill me, they stumble and fall.
> Even if a whole army surrounds me, I will not be afraid; even if enemies attack me, I will still trust God.

I have asked the Lord for one thing; one thing only do I want: to live in the Lord's house all my life, to marvel there at his goodness, and to ask his guidance.

In times of trouble he will shelter me; he will keep me safe in his Temple and make me secure on a high rock. . . .

My father and mother may abandon me, but the Lord will take care of me.

Psalm 27:1–5, 10, TEV

4

Anger
The Two-Edged Sword

> When my father left
> I was two weeks old
> I never really knew him.
> Of all the fathers on this earth.
> I'm sorry that I drew him.

O h! The awful things we do when we are angry. Sometimes we don't even bother to figure out with whom we are angry. We let it flash out in all directions like a Fourth of July sparkler. With angry words or acts of retaliation, we attack and wound others for real or imagined injuries inflicted on us.

Anger Is Self-Destructive

But anger can be even more dangerous when teenagers find ways to get back at their parents that are far more injurious to themselves than to the parents. Alison ran away. Deb stopped eating. Bill started smoking pot. Dan tried booze. Carey began shoplifting. Frank started fights with everybody. Jamie became sexually promiscuous.

Each of these young people was extremely angry and allowed that anger to be a self-destructive force. Yes, their parents were hurt, too. But the long-lasting damage was to the teenager.

Alison

Furious with her divorced mother for being too busy with her new male friends—she never had time for her daughter anymore—Alison left home. She was going to hitchhike from Michigan to California to see her dad and had no difficulty getting rides. But Alison was raped and beaten to death. They found her body in a dump. She was fourteen.

Deb

What Deb needed was to be more in control of her life. Because there was nothing she could do about her parents' situation, she felt helpless. Deb was determined to control at least her own body. Although exercising obsessively, she practically stopped eating. By the time her stepmother noticed, this 5'5" girl had dropped from 120 to 96 pounds. In spite of urging and pleading from her parents, she continued to lose weight until at a frail 87 pounds she was admitted to the hospital for tubal feeding. After eight months in a psychiatric facility, Deb is home again, but her physical system has been seriously stressed.

The rising incidence of anorexia nervosa (and its related eating disorder, bulimia—the binging-purging syndrome) is evidence that more and more teenagers, especially girls, are taking out their frustrations and self-image problems on their own bodies. There is almost always an emotional basis for their disorders. If being ever-thinner has become a compulsion for you, so that you find it increasingly difficult to consume enough food to maintain your health, seek help immediately!

Bill

He started with the pot as an experimental kick, but Bill stayed with it because it gave him a pleasant hazy apathy through which his family problems did not look so bad. But Bill was short of cash to support his habit and got busted for breaking and entering. He has been through juvenile-detention proceedings and two group homes.

Dan

A member of A.A. and a recovering alcoholic, Dan can tell you, "I will never be able to take even one drink." He is sixteen. His liver is permanently damaged.

Carey

This teenage girl, too, has been through the juvenile-court system. Carey is still living at home but she reports to her parole officer regularly. She was seventeen when she was last arrested for shoplifting—her third offense. So she was tried as an adult and now has a criminal record.

Frank

A real rebel was Frank. He struck out at everyone and everything. His gang got into a rumble and a sixteen-year-old member of another gang was killed. Frank is now doing time in the penitentiary.

Jamie

Reacting in anger to the infidelity of her pious, church-going mother, Jamie brought her first sexual partner home to play in her parents' bed while they were on vacation. Several sexual encounters later, she discovered she was pregnant and had also contracted herpes.

All of these kids were acting out anger related to their parents' separation, divorce, and various remarriages. They chose—perhaps unconsciously—terribly destructive behaviors, resulting in serious physical and psychological damage with long-lasting effects.

To Be Angry Is Not a Sin

You may be angry at one or both of your parents. They have upset the status quo. They are forcing you to make choices you do not want to make. There will be changes in your lifestyle and your financial situation.

You might have had dreams for the future which you have not yet discussed with anyone. Some of these dreams had to do with your education and your plans for a career. Maybe they were about vacations you hoped your family could take together. Of course, those dreams of yours might not have worked out, anyhow. But it seems certain they cannot materialize now. And so you are angry at your parents because you see it as their fault that your plans have gone down the tube. How disillusioning! Didn't they owe you that much? Why did they have you or adopt you if they couldn't stay together to provide you with your dream?

You cannot help being angry. Anger is a primitive emotion that all of us experience. In fact, when we are threatened, anger triggers necessary physiological changes such as increased heartbeat and the release of energy-heightening substances in our bloodstream, all of which prepare us for defense. In less "civilized" times, anger was a factor in self-preservation. Anger itself is no more destructive than any other emotion. It is not wrong or bad to feel angry. To be angry is not a sin.

But you could get into trouble by letting your anger control you. Anger is like the steam that forms in a pot of boiling water. If the pot has a tight lid, the steam builds up until it blows off the lid.

Then it is destructive. But if the lid has a vent, the steam has a safely controlled way to escape.

The safest way to vent anger is to talk about it. If possible, talk about it with the person toward whom the anger is directed. That may not always be feasible. But it is necessary to talk to someone.

Anger, like steam, will continue to build if it remains close to the heat. It may be necessary for you to get away from the source of your anger and talk your head of steam down to a safe level before you try to talk to your parent(s).

Find a Listener

You need a friend who listens and does not give out a lot of unsolicited advice. Although you are really a pretty smart person and can figure out a lot of things for yourself, it helps to bounce your ideas off someone else. Religious leaders are often good listeners. This includes pastors, priests, youth workers, and Sunday school teachers. Other persons who might be helpful are teachers, scout leaders, or maybe even a grandparent.

When looking for a sympathetic listener, look for an understanding head nodder who lets you do the talking. Avoid preachy sermonizers. Friends your own age can be valuable sounding boards. You may find that just verbalizing your angry feelings will put them in a new perspective in your life.

Bert

"The thing that helped me the most was my friends," said Bert. "I could hang around them and at times I'd forget all about the divorce. It was a tough time, but being around them kind of cleared my mind and made it easier to come back to the house. I was really active in sports and that helped because then I could achieve for myself and that helped with other things."

Bert was on to something important. Physical activity is another vent in the pot lid. You might try jogging, golfing, swimming, or pounding a punching bag. If there is no opportunity for any of these activities, try pounding your pillow with a newspaper. (Somehow noise seems to help.) It is certainly less destructive than beating your head against the wall!

How Can You Be Angry with Someone You Love?

Sometimes kids think it is wrong to be angry with their parents. But they are, and then they feel guilty because they are angry. This can lead to an overwhelming sadness. Then they get angry with themselves for being so sad—and around and around they go. This is a dangerous whirlpool that can suck you into some of that destructive behavior described earlier.

Being angry at someone does not mean that you do not love him or her. In fact, you will get even more angry at people you love, because when you love others you feel close to them. You trust them. When they do something that hurts, you feel betrayed, and you are furious with them for letting you down. One of the reasons some people get caught up in self-destructive behaviors is that they are angry at themselves for being so vulnerable to the hurt. They left themselves open by being trusting. On the other hand, people you do not particularly care about lack the capability to make you really angry. That is because you do not really care if they do something to create distance between you.

Handling Your Anger

So, what are you going to do with all of this anger—to keep it from taking over and destroying you? We have mentioned venting your emotion by talking. Moving away from the source of the anger reduces its intensity, but it is still there below the surface. The only way to get rid of your anger safely and totally is to forgive. Wow! That's a big order, isn't it?

Paul, in his letter to the Ephesians, gave us a formula worthy of consideration. We read:

> Get rid of all bitterness, passion, and anger. No more shouting or insults, no more hateful feelings of any sort. Instead, be kind and tender-hearted to one another, and forgive one another, as God has forgiven you through Christ.
>
> Ephesians 4:31–32, TEV

I doubt that Paul expected anyone to accomplish all this overnight. But you can get started on it. Forgiving is a verb—something you actively do. Forgiveness does not just happen if you wait long enough.

Think about the wrongs (either real or imagined) that you have experienced. Talk about them with one or both of your parents if possible. Listen to their feedback as well. Repeat over and over to yourself, "I can forgive Mom [or Dad] for that." When you finally believe that, you will feel a great relief. It will help if you can tell your parents, too. If you find that too difficult, at least tell them how much you love them. And once you have forgiven them, you will find yourself able to be more loving. Ask God to help you. Remember, He has had a lot of experience in the forgiving department:

> Two other men, both of them criminals, were also led out to be put to death with Jesus. When they came to the place called "The Skull," they crucified Jesus there, and the two criminals, one on his right and the other on his left. Jesus said, "Forgive them, Father! They don't know what they are doing."
>
> Luke 23:32–34, TEV

Anger is an emotion that is part of our makeup because God planned it that way. But God meant for us to control our anger and channel it into constructive action and forgiveness—not for our anger to control us.

5

Grief
Mourning the Loss

> Did you ever hear the whistle
> of a far off train
> And wish that you were on it
> and feel a sort of pain?
> Like something's lost or gone
> that can never come back again.
>
> I saw the judge in his black gown.
> I heard him bang the gavel down.
> I heard the whistle through the town.

There is a lot of grief associated with divorce. Every member of the family experiences it, as there are many losses to be mourned. Grief can be and often is expressed in different ways, but unless it is dealt with openly it will act like a cancer eating away at your spirit. And it can leave you an emotional cripple.

One or both of your parents may be grieving for the lost love, for the shattered relationship, or for the loss of esteem that goes with being half of a couple. As they grieve for the loss of their identity as a wife or husband, their whole image of their own personhood is altered and usually warped.

The parent who does not get custody will probably grieve the loss of parenting privileges and the opportunity to share fully in his or her children's day-to-day experiences.

With all of this parental hurt, don't be surprised if there seems a lack of sensitivity to your grief or little energy to help you cope. Remember, others in the family are struggling grimly to keep from drowning in their own sea of tears.

The Announcement of the Divorce

All of the young people I interviewed had one thing in common. They remembered with agonizing clarity the announcement of their parents' divorce, even though several years had elapsed since. They could recall their reactions vividly.

Chris

Remembers Chris, "It was my mother's birthday. I thought it was awful."

Andy

"I couldn't handle it that first night," said Andy. "I went to one of the elders and he helped me to get hold of myself. He got me to sit down and talk about it. So at least I wasn't all shaken up about it anymore. But it hurt. I hurt for an awful long time and I still do. And the hurt is an actual physical pain."

Gloria

So acute was Gloria's distress that she ran immediately to the bathroom and began to vomit. She reports, "I had trouble catching my breath and my heart was racing a hundred miles an hour."

The Pain Lingers

Even after the initial shock is past, the pain and sense of loss remain, sometimes for years after the actual divorce. What once was is gone, probably forever—the closeness of the family circle, the security of being part of a whole loving unit, the memories of holiday gatherings.

Betsy

Because Betsy's father left when she was only eight days old, she grew up with a strong bond of closeness with her grandfather. When she was sixteen her grandfather died, and Betsy's grief for her lost father-figure was accentuated by her mourning the relationship with a real father she never had. She said, "My father's more of an acquaintance. Not close. He's interested in me and I tell him about what I'm doing in my life. Just general things. Very general. No feelings."

Andy

Grief is not just for yourself and your own losses. Andy was very much caught up in the dynamics of what was happening to other members of his family, and some of his deep sadness was for them.

"I am reminded of it often, and things my father has done since bother me. He's already moved in with another woman and is planning to marry her as soon as both of their respective divorces are finally settled. So it is an ongoing pain. I could understand that there were problems in the marriage. I can't understand why my dad had to go right away to this other person. I love both of my parents, and I wanted to say to Dad, 'What are you doing to yourself? Why are you going to plunge right into this when you don't even know exactly what it is that happened between you and Mom?'"

Marie

Although now at college, Marie grieves the loss of a "whole family," the going home to visit her mom and dad: "Because I'm so far away from home, the few times I go home are very special. My best memories of 'family' are of Christmas, because we always got together in those huge family gatherings with all the relatives and tons of food and fun and presents. And all of a sudden my mother is odd-woman-out. She's a divorced lady and it's all very hush-hush. We're just a little bit apart and there's sort of a little wall. Nobody says anything. Nobody does anything, but there's just sort of a distance. So I've lost the closeness of Christmases that I really valued."

The Shame of Divorce

The mourning of a parental divorce is related to a sense of rejection, of unlovability, of embarrassment. Children of all ages tend to conclude secretly, "My parent left because I was unlovable." Even where no such thoughts occur, a sense of shame can further heighten the feeling of loss.

Marie

"I was so ashamed," continued Marie. "I had always thought of myself as a liberal, and yet I was ashamed that my parents had gotten a divorce. I had a very close friend whom I'd kept in touch with since high school, though we'd gone to different colleges. Yet, I was ashamed to tell her that my parents had gotten a divorce. It took me three months—I mean, the whole summer in which I'd been going through all this. She was my very best friend in whom I should have confided on day one. But I didn't even tell her until three months had gone by."

Chuck

When Chuck's friend asked why his dad was not around,

Chuck had a different answer every time. "Working overtime." "Gone to a meeting." "Extra training sessions." He could not bring himself to tell his best friend that his father had left the family.

Rob

Only seven when his parents were divorced, Rob was so successful at repressing his distress that he "forgot" to tell his fiancée that his parents had been divorced. Rob told her that his father had died a few months before they met, and this *was* true. But it was only after they had been married several years that Rob's wife learned from her mother-in-law about the divorce.

Reacting to the Pain

There are as many different ways of reacting to the pain of parental divorce as there are personalities and prior experiences for the individuals involved.

Janyce

The grieving was double-barreled for Janyce. Her parents' marriage had been a stormy one for some time. She was almost relieved when her father left, because the pressure was off at home. But then she thought, "Whoa! What am I saying? This is wrong." So she was feeling guilty about that. And then her father died very suddenly, one month before the divorce was to be final.

Janyce began to grieve when she saw her father's body. She mourned his death, the loss of a father, and the separation they had experienced. All of this was overwhelming and she became withdrawn from her friends. Her school grades suffered. As she put it, "I didn't really participate. I just lost contact with everything. I didn't think I belonged anymore. I didn't think they'd want to hear about my problems. I thought they wouldn't understand. They'd just want to leave me alone or something. But my friends kind of stood around and waited. And they understood."

Bert

"It was a relief to know it was all over," said Bert. "But then I'd think about that piece of paper sitting there and I'd remember our family and how it had been, with the trips and vacations. It's still sometimes hard to believe it. When I look back to when I was five and six and seven, I think we had a pretty solid family. We did things together—fun things like camping, vacation trips, picking blueberries. I figured we had a pretty normal, together kind of a family that would always be like that. Only now it's not."

Barb

For Barb: "In one way I think it would have been easier if one of them had just died. There would have been no one to blame. That person would be completely gone. The pain could heal. This way I'm always torn, and the wound is always open. You get used to it after a while like there's a scab on it, but then something happens to scratch the scab off and you find yourself bleeding again."

Divorce Is the Death of a Family

The grief over a divorce is very much like the mourning period after a death. In fact, there has been a death—the death of a family. There is a hole in what once was a whole. As with any death, it is appropriate to grieve.

Grief often occurs in distinct stages, each with its own characteristic dominant emotion. In fact, professionals who have studied the mourning process believe that passage through some or all of the stages is important if total healing is to occur.

1. Denial: The first stage of grief is usually denial. Nearly every one of the young people reported that even though they knew their parents' marriage was unstable or was suddenly in serious trouble, they did not really believe they would divorce.

Chris

Although her father had been receiving treatment at a mental-health center and her mother had been a patient, too, Chris said, "I guess I didn't want it to happen, so I didn't think about it. And, no, I wasn't ready for it."

Many teenagers admit that right up until the divorce was final they toyed with the fantasy that "maybe, somehow" their folks would get back together again. For some the fantasy continued even after one or both parents had remarried.

2. Bargaining: Another stage in the grief process is bargaining with parents, or even with God. "Why me? I'll be good . . ." This is usually played out by kids who feel that somehow the divorce is their fault. So they become models of good behavior. They reason, "If Dad [Mom] left because I was so awful, I'll be as good as I can and maybe he [she] will come back." Often this form of bargaining is not only ineffective, it is unnoticed. Parents who are struggling with their own grief and conflicting emotions tend to lose their sensitivity toward others. If someone asks how the kids are doing, the parent may respond, "Much better than I am. They seem much happier and are doing fine." When it becomes apparent to the teenager that this type of bargaining is ineffective, another stage of grief—anger—may be entered. Anger is so all-consuming and so common that it has its own chapter. Read about anger in chapter four.

3. Depression: Sadness or depression is what most persons think of first, when they hear the word *grief*. A lot of sadness is associated with the divorce of your parents, and this stage of the grief process is probably most prevalent and painful. You cry, either alone or with your brothers and sisters. Sometimes you cry with one or both of your parents.

But some of the time you wish you could cry and the tears do not come. There is only a dry lump in your throat that will not budge. Either it is so big that you have a hard time swallowing—so that you don't eat very much at all—or you start eating and hope that with the next swallow the lump will be gone.

There is a heavy weight on your chest. It feels as if the fat lady from the circus is sitting on you. Or maybe a big rock seems to be perched on your shoulders. It is hard to believe such physical pain and its source are not visible to others.

It is not easy to be with people when you feel like this. You believe that your sadness shows all over you, and you would not want to spoil other people's good times.

Chuck

As Chuck described this feeling, "There's no fun in my life anymore." He recounted the many sadnesses he was experiencing. "Dad says he doesn't have very much money. The rest of us don't have very much money, either. It's hard to concentrate on school work. I have a paper due Tuesday, but I have to have it done before Monday or else Mom won't have time to type it. She's working now. It's camping season but we can't go." As his list went on he looked sadder by the minute.

You could be having sleep problems, too, as part of your depression. Maybe you go to sleep okay, but you wake up early and cannot go back to sleep, and you lie there thinking about how awful life is. Or maybe you have dreams about the family and being back together. These are almost worse than the occasional nightmares, because it is such a disappointment when you wake up to reality.

4. Acceptance: The final stage of grief is acceptance. It is one thing to accept in your mind that your parents do not love each other anymore and that some changes have to be made. It is possible to acknowledge that these changes may include a different place to live, Mom's going to work, not seeing one of your parents so often, and less money for living expenses. But the hard reality comes when you realize that these changes are permanent. Things will never, ever, be like they were before. If that sentence brings tears to your eyes, read it again. Read it until you know in your heart that it is true. Only then can you begin to heal from the deep hurt of your parents' divorce.

Marie

Eventually, Marie was able to say, "Aren't I the same person I was before? My parents got divorced. I didn't. My father is still my father and my mother is still my mother. Nothing has changed in my relationship to them. Their relationship has changed. After eight years, I have a better perspective on it and age does something for you."

Recurrent Grief

Just when you think you have pretty well accepted the loss and settled your grief, something comes up to set you back. It may be something special you wish the whole family could share together, such as your solo in the concert or your award at the art show. Or, it could be your graduation, a scholarship award, or even your wedding. And there you are—stuck with only one parent or the dilemma of how to juggle two people who both love you, but who are not very friendly toward each other. Expect those relapses. They are a normal, very human part of your mourning mechanism.

The Healing Process

Part of your total healing comes from talking to people over and over and over, until you can live with the finality of the divorce and your emotions. Sometimes you cannot hear your hurt until you put it into words.

Barb

It was hard for Barb to talk to religious leaders because "I was so angry at God. It was important for me to stay around healthy people and not get caught up in other people's war stories. It was supportive to be with friends who reminded me of my strengths."

The Bible has some words of comfort for the grieving. David the psalmist gives an accurate picture of how the pain of grief feels, and he describes it:

> I am worn out, O Lord; have pity on me!
> Give me strength; I am completely exhausted, and my whole being is deeply troubled.
> How long, O Lord, will you wait to help me?
> Come and save me, Lord; in your mercy rescue me from death.
> In the world of the dead you are not remembered; no one can praise you there.
> I am worn out with grief; every night my bed is damp from my weeping; my pillow is soaked with tears.
> I can hardly see; my eyes are so swollen from the weeping caused by my enemies.
>
> Psalm 6:2–7, TEV

Christ, in His death on the cross, experienced separation from His Father. And in His anguish He cried, "My God, why have your deserted me?" (Mark 15:34, LB).

Having experienced this kind of grief, He sends a comforting promise of peace:

> Don't worry about anything, but in all your prayers ask God for what you need, always asking him with a thankful heart. And God's peace, which is far beyond human understanding, will keep your hearts and minds safe in union with Christ Jesus.
>
> Philippians 4:6–7, TEV

Let us be bold, then, and say, "The Lord is my helper. I will not be afraid. What can anyone do to me?" Remember your former leaders, who spoke God's message to you. Think back on how they lived and died, and imitate their faith. Jesus Christ is the same yesterday, today, and forever.

Hebrews 13:6–8, TEV

Here is one other word to the grieving, from Proverbs 17:22: "Being cheerful keeps you healthy. It is slow death to be gloomy all the time" (TEV).

6

In the Middle
I Feel Like a Ping-Pong Ball

>They are vying for points.
>Mom tries to put on a little English
>While Dad maneuvers for a smash
>That will hit just the other side of the net.
>They are worthy opponents
>But neither loses well.
>And as I ricochet from slap to slam
>My head is really spinning.
>One toss-up for us all—
>Is anyone really winning?

Some parents have a hard time giving up the battle. It seems as though they have agreed to disagree—on everything—forever. So the battle goes on over who gets what, the amount of support, visitation rights, and a score of other details. And you are caught smack-bang in the middle. If you mention anything that sounds like support of one parent, you open yourself to a lecture from the other, outlining the former partner's many sins of omission and commission.

When Parents Probe

You may be questioned about everything from financial situations—"Has your dad said anything about a raise?" "How could your mother afford a car? Is she getting money someplace else?"—to personal behavior—"I suppose he had a girlfriend with him." Or, "What's her boyfriend like?"

This is an extremely uncomfortable position for you. Although your parents have severed their marital relationship, the emotional ties and wounds are still there. Often their quest for information is merely to arm themselves for further battle.

The best solution for you is to say nothing to either parent about the other's behavior, finances, or friends. It is unfair of them to expect you to be a go-between. It is their battle, not yours, and you should stay out of it if at all possible.

This calls for maturity and assertiveness. It may be necessary to say, "If you and Dad [Mom] want to discuss that, you'll have to talk to each other." Or, "I am uncomfortable reporting to you on my other parent. I wish you wouldn't ask me to do that."

Kids Can Be the Battlefield for the Parents' War

There are bound to be emotional scars whenever children are used as a battleground for warring parents. Either or both parents may be demanding your loyalty. Even if your parents are not pressuring you, you may find reasons to take sides or feel guilty. You live in a constant state of tension, knowing that every move you make will have an effect on both households and may cause you to feel disloyal to one or the other parent.

One game divorced parents have played with younger children is for the custodial parent to send the kids to visit the other parent in old, wornout clothing, as if to say, "See how poor we are?" Some noncustodial parents have responded to this ploy by buying new clothes, toys, or other items and keeping them at their house in readiness for the children's visits.

Penny

Although her parents divorced when she was only six, Penny, at age nineteen, reports that her parents are still fighting over their children. "The court decided we were to live with my mother, but we had to go visit my father for a month every summer or else two weeks at Christmas. We kids didn't like it. My father and stepmother would say things, and we would go back and repeat them. My mother didn't like it, and she'd say things, and we'd go back over there and repeat that. It was a disaster area.

"At my dad's there was always a lot of everything: good food, toys, clothes. And we loved it. But then we had to go back to nothing again, and our stepbrother and half-sister had everything, including our father. That was very hard. Dad would pay only the minimal amount of support that he could get away with, yet he always demanded his visitation rights. Quite a few times I said, 'Life is not fair.'"

Tom

While Tom lived with his mom, she remained very angry with his father although the divorce had been final for five years. Tom's contacts with his father had been infrequent and complicated by stormy scenes with his mother. Whenever Tom mentioned wanting to see Dad, Mom went into an angry tirade saying things like, "I don't know why you even bring it up. You know he doesn't want anything to do with us. He'll only slap you around, anyway. Don't even bring it up again."

But, with the help and encouragement of a counselor, Tom gained enough courage to mention it again and did make the contact with his dad. Since Mom needed a lot of professional help to get over this crisis, Tom was able to spend time with his father and see him in a new light—not just through Mom's eyes. He found that Dad was not the "awful ogre" that Mom had painted him to be. Nor was he the perfectly wonderful Mr. Nice Guy that Tom had fantasized. The truth of who his dad really was lay somewhere in the murky middle.

It is courageous and even daring to decline to be a part of your parents' little war games. It is necessary, however, for the preservation of your own sanity and good feelings about yourself to remember whose battle it is and stay out of it. Give neither of them any fuel for their fire.

Honesty Is Still the Best Policy

You may be tempted to slant information given to one parent so as to please and win the approval of the parent who hears it. Since it is never possible to be entirely sure how such information will be received and interpreted, even the best of intentions can lead you astray. It is better not to say anything about one parent to the other. Encourage each of them to speak directly to the other if there is business to discuss or arrangements to be made. This will reduce the chance of your getting the blame when one of them misunderstands or does not like what the other one says.

Another no-win strategy that might appeal to you is to play one parent against the other to your own advantage. You might even justify doing this, since you feel their divorce is unfair to you. But in your heart you will know such divisive behavior is wrong, and wrongdoing engaged in deliberately creates guilt. You don't need any more misery right now! So be honest and up front with your parents. Require them to be responsible for their own communications with each other. Feel free to align yourself on specific issues with one or the other of your parents as you choose. But do not allow them to keep you "in the middle."

Your Image of Your Parent Molds Your Own Self-Image

Sometimes a parent is so angry at the ex-spouse that he or she habitually bad-mouths the absent parent to the child. If one or both of your parents is doing this to you, and you allow it to continue, it will have a negative effect on your own self-image.

If you had both a beaker of used automotive oil and a beaker of milk and poured some of each into a third beaker, you would have a real mess! Likewise, if one parent, no matter how pure and nurturing, continues to portray the other half of your heritage as nasty, ugly, and worthless, you may come to see yourself as unable to be anything other than "a mess."

For your own self-esteem—as well as in the interests of fair play—it is important that you not listen to one parent run the other one down. You may have to be very direct. You may need to say something like, "I don't like to hear you talking badly about my other parent. When you do that you make me feel bad, too, because I am a child of each of you. I know you two are angry at each other, but I don't want to hear how awful you think that other person is."

"Nice Parents" vs. "Mean Parent"

It will be easy to begin to see the parent you live with as the villain and the visiting parent as Mr. Nice Guy or Mrs. Wonderful. Just living in the same house with someone, especially the disciplinarian who makes and enforces the house rules, is going to create some friction. There are probably extra chores and less money, which means more work for you with less rewards. This situation can create some arguments and fussing between you and your "home" parent, who is probably already extra tired from doubling as wage earner and housekeeper.

The noncustodial parent, on the other hand, arrives on a day off from work and—wanting to please—buys meals of your choice and provides fun trips to amusement parks and game rooms or visits to his or her new home, which may be more lavish than the one in which you now live.

Be fair! Don't let all those good times and treats let you forget that the parent with whom you live on a regular basis might like to provide such special extras, too, but is unable to afford the outlay of the necessary time and money.

How Much Responsibility Should You Assume?

There are times when you will feel older than your years as you consider the characteristic "burdens" and emotions which are part of the territory of being a child of divorce. You may face emotions and decisions not usually encountered by a teenager and wonder how much you are expected to handle.

Bert

"Dad is lonely," Bert observed. "I try to go there every weekend, but I've got a lot of stuff going on, too. I figure he's got to start making his own new life. He's got to start finding a girlfriend or wife. I know he likes us kids a lot, but I've got to be getting on with my life, too."

Gina

When she was only five years old, Gina's parents divorced, and it was a messy divorce. There had been some spouse and child abuse, and there were many false and unkind accusations. The finalizing of the divorce was delayed by all the allegations and defenses.

Before the divorce was final, Gina's mother had begun to date another man whom she married soon after the divorce. This was a warm and loving man who became a good father to Gina and her younger brother and sister. There was a lot of affection between the children and their new stepfather, and a happy home life was in the making.

But Gina's natural father continued to want his visitation privileges, even though his support payments were late in coming or did not come at all. In addition, the visits were painful for the children, who were subjected to stories of their mother's imagined misdeeds. They were also fearful of their father because of his threats and actual abuse in the past.

Gina felt truly loved the day her stepfather took control of the situation and said to her natural father, "Here's the deal, you don't have to pay any more support, but you see the kids only on their birthdays and at Christmas and on my terms." When her father readily agreed to this, Gina felt relief. It was evident to her which man was truly the loving father, and she felt safe with him. She was very pleased when her stepfather initiated the move to adopt the three of them.

Unfortunately, tragedy struck. When Gina was fourteen years old, her mother died in an automobile accident. There had been two more children born to the family and Gina was now thrust into the role of "little mother" for four younger children. She and her stepfather became even more close and he relied on her heavily.

Since Gina loved him very much, she rejoiced for him when he found another woman to marry. He assured her that he had loved her mother very much and hoped his remarriage would help him recapture some of his former happiness.

Conflict for Gina arose because the new stepmother appeared jealous of the close relationship which Gina had with her stepfather. Gina was uncomfortably in the middle. It was hard for her to relinquish the caring, nurturing role toward her younger siblings. While this nurturing of the younger children was appreciated by her stepfather, it only drove a wider wedge between Gina and his wife. The harder Gina tried for her love and approval, the more rejection she experienced. But Gina has a success story.

After ten years, the gap began to heal, as her stepmother finally recognized that neither Gina nor the other children were threats to her marriage relationship with their father.

But this alienation was healed only because of Gina's continual loving efforts to heal the gap. She opened herself to hurt time and time again and came back after experiencing repeated rejections.

Still feel like a Ping-Pong ball? I suspect there are a variety of ways to be caught in the middle. You are pulled between two parents who both feel entitled to your love and support. It will probably be helpful to talk to someone else—a trusted friend, wise adult, or understanding advisor—to help you gain some other perspectives on your situation. And even when you feel that you are being torn in two, read this Psalm of David to remind you of that Special Someone who is always there:

> God is our shelter and strength, always ready to help in times of trouble.
> So we will not be afraid, even if the earth is shaken and mountains fall into the ocean depths; even if the seas roar and rage, and the hills are shaken by the violence.
> There is a river that brings joy to the city of God, to the sacred house of the Most High.
> God is in that city, and it will never be destroyed; at early dawn he will come to its aid.
> Nations are terrified, kingdoms are shaken; God thunders, and the earth dissolves.
> The Lord Almighty is with us; the God of Jacob is our refuge.
>
> Psalm 46:1–7, TEV

7

Switching Roles
I Don't Want to Be the Parent

> I caught a glimpse of her
> Through the half-open door
> Frighteningly alluring.
> Taking a deep breath
> I firmly closed the door
> On temptation and returned
> To my game of checkers.

Sometimes parents who find themselves without a spouse feel overwhelmed with all the responsibility of being the head of the house. As they look around for someone with whom to share this responsibility, they frequently choose the oldest child of the opposite sex to fill the shoes of the missing marital partner.

Or the child may assume this role voluntarily, taking on the responsibility out of a sense of duty and feeling, "It's the least I can do." For whatever reason, suddenly you find yourself the "man of the house" or the "little mother."

The role may have a certain appeal, at least at first. It brings with it an added sense of importance, and it certainly helps to avoid, at least temporarily, that feeling of helplessness most kids experience when their parents' marriage is falling apart.

You gradually (or suddenly) assume duties that would not otherwise be yours. Some of these might be: responsibility for younger children, meal preparation, and care and maintenance of the family car. Of course, you might have been expected to help with these tasks even if your family had stayed together. However, if they are requiring larger chunks of your day or there is no time for normal youthful pursuits, there may be a problem.

Substitute Spouse Is Not a Healthy Teenage Role

If your custodial parent is turning to you more and more for advice and input on adult decisions, this may be very flattering. But it may not be the healthiest situation in the world for either of you.

Some parents, during the first pains of a failed marriage, regress to the point where they are not even able to care for themselves adequately. Decision-making abilities fly out the window as they become "children" themselves, dependent on anyone who will function in their behalf. It is often the older children in the family who slip into the caretaker role.

Such demonstrations of caring and support for a hurting parent are surely helpful and appreciated, but you should not have to continue in this role for an extended period of time.

Kids are often frightened and confused when they see evidence that their parent is unable to put it together after a crisis such as divorce. The crisis itself is rocking the boat, but when there is no parental stability the boat is in real danger of being swamped altogether.

Some teenagers choose to bail out of the family boat at this point. They run away from home. Or they stay but become family drop-outs, spending most of their time somewhere else. In their search for control, they are vulnerable to cults or antisocial groups where leadership is strong and controls are rigid.

The Burden of Being Responsible

Other kids choose to take over the helm and steer a course for less troubled waters. While this is an admirable action, it requires a great deal of responsibility and, for the time being, keeps the teenager from his or her own pursuits.

This sense of responsibility for the parent, once assumed, may persist even after the crisis is over. Just as it is necessary for parents to emancipate their teens, who thus become adults, so must teenagers be able to separate and discontinue the over-protection and "parenting" of their parents. Otherwise, the "captain" may never again assume command of the boat.

Bert

Remember Bert from the previous chapter? Bert said, "I feel so sorry for Dad. He's lost everything. I still have my mom and my sister and now my mom's boyfriend. And we still have the house. But I feel so sorry for him because he's all alone. I want to be over there, but then I can't all the time. I've got to live my life, and he's got to live his. That's the only way I can look at it."

Marisa

After Marisa's father left, her mother began to drink heavily. More and more of the household responsibility and care of two younger children fell to Marisa. She said, "I kept thinking that Mom would snap out of it. I knew it was tough for her. I wanted to get out, too. But I was worried about the younger kids. If I said anything to my mom about her drinking, she'd cry and say she was sorry and it would be better for a few days. Then it would be worse than ever. I was afraid to tell my dad because I knew he'd only get mad and make more trouble. I finally talked to my aunt, my mom's sister, and she talked my mom into going to A.A. Things are pretty good now. I even have friends over to the house again."

Todd

It was Todd's mother who pushed him into the role of man of the house after the divorce. Todd said, "At first it was okay. I did stuff like taking down screens and cleaning the rain gutters. I used to help with that anyhow. But then I was supposed to fix anything that went wrong with the car and I didn't know everything about that. I was only fifteen. Then Mom got to where she wouldn't go any place without me. I felt kinda dumb about that. 'Specially when I would be the only kid there. The real trouble came when I met this girl I like. We were on vacation. My mom started acting really cranky and I didn't know what was going on 'till I figured out she was jealous and I thought 'Oh, no! Now what?' That's when I knew I had to find somebody else to talk to."

Resentment Builds

Having to assume a parent's share of responsibility can build a lot of resentment, which is not good for family relationships or for any of the individuals involved.

Penny

Because her mother had to work, Penny had to watch her two younger brothers after school. She felt very put upon because she was the oldest and a girl, and she felt her two brothers got away with doing nothing. "My little brother has allergies to everything and I have to be the one to give him a shot of adrenalin, and it's tough. I was glad to get away to camp and now to college."

While such responsibility may be flattering for a while and a heady ego trip for some kids, for others it is awesomely overwhelming. So they respond with self-destructive and/or antisocial behaviors that are both attention seeking and a cry for someone else to take control. Abuse of alcohol and other drugs, gang fighting, and larceny will get attention, all right! But this type of behavior can leave you with some feelings about yourself that are not very good.

Steve

Since Steve's mother was a nurse, her hours were not regular, and she worked some days and some evenings. She relied on Steve, who was fourteen, to keep an eye on his twelve-year-old brother and ten-year-old sister. Because his mother's schedule was unpredictable, Steve could not get involved in an organized sports group. He did, however, invite friends to the house in her absence.

Steve says: "I know now it was dumb, but we got into pot. When my mom was gone we spent long, lazy afternoons and evenings completely stoned. She caught on when one of the guys started stealing stuff from our place. By then I was not much concerned about my family anymore. I only wanted what felt good for me. My mom and I had a big hassle. She tried to make me feel guilty by telling me she needed me. I said a lot of dumb things. I remember saying, 'Well, I don't need you.' I moved out for a while and stayed with my aunt and uncle, but after about six months I got my head on straight and moved back home. My mom and I still have arguments sometimes, but she lets me be a kid more. I try to do my share, so it is better now."

Incest

Sexual involvement of a parent with his or her child may occur even in homes where there has been no divorce or separation. It is an even graver problem in a single-parent household, where the victim has no access to the other parent who might otherwise be there to protect the child and see that the behavior stops.

Kelly

When Kelly's mother died, her dad began to idolize Kelly. He gave her a lot of privileges and treated her like someone very special. Kelly was flattered by all of the royal treatment:

"He kept saying I was just like my mother and he really loved me. But then I found out he wanted me to be a sexual partner, too. At first it was just little things. A pat here or a touch there, and he was so good to me—but then it got more and more involved. I was really mixed up because he kept saying it was okay and he never hurt me. But I started feeling really guilty and I couldn't talk about it with even my best girlfriend. When I thought I was pregnant I went to Planned Parenthood for a pregnancy test and a counselor there really helped me to know I needed a lot more help."

Unfortunately, sexual molestation of young children and teenagers by a parent or stepparent is occurring more frequently, or at least is being reported more often, now that the subject of incest has lost some of its hush-hush character. Incidentally, incestuous behavior with a stepparent may seem to be less serious an offense because the adult is not a blood relative—at least that is the sales pitch a stepparent may make to his or her victim. However, the behavior is still very wrong! If a stepparent has even *tried* to involve you in sexual acts, tell the other parent immediately. This may seem difficult for you to do, especially since the other parent may initially disbelieve you.

Sexual involvement of a minor with an adult is always wrong—and it is even more so when it concerns parent and child, no matter how "innocent" a picture the offending adult may paint. If you are living with just one parent and cannot stop that parent's sexual advances with a firm "No!"—even if the parent has threatened reprisals if you confide in someone else—leave the house as soon as possible and seek refuge in the home of a nearby relative or friend. Your only recourse may be to report directly to the juvenile authorities, who can help you contact your noncustodial parent (if you have one), or will find a foster placement for you and any younger brothers and sisters who may also have been victimized. Remember that you, as a minor, are the victim, not the offender, even though you have been persuaded to take part in a parent's sexual activities. Although the parent may need help, too, yours is the immediate need.

There are support groups in some localities which have been helpful to many incest victims. If there is none nearby, seek counsel with your family doctor, minister, or even a school advisor. The sooner after the initial event that you seek help, the better will be the outcome for all concerned. Delaying because of embarrassment, fear, or other emotions will only prolong your suffering and guilt feelings. If there seems to be no other avenue of escape, phone the emergency room of the local hospital. (In most cases, you will not have to give your name.) The hospital personnel should be able to provide you with the number of a support group or individual in the area.

Keep Responsibility in Balance

There are plenty of problems to be encountered in normal adolescence. Gradual separation from the family nest so that you can become an independent, responsible adult is one of the challenges of your teenage years. While being "responsible" may mean helping out at home, it should not be necessary for you to function as a spouse to your single parent.

A parent who is making such overwhelming demands on you may not even be aware of the stress being placed on you. Or your parent may acknowledge the strain but expect you to carry on anyway. No matter how much love you share, you feel trapped, because this is a parent you should be able to trust to make good decisions in your behalf as well as handle his or her own affairs as an adult.

David the psalmist experienced betrayal by someone whom he trusted. He describes his anguish and turns to God for solace:

> If it were an enemy making fun of me, I could endure it; if it were an opponent boasting over me, I could hide myself from him.
> But it is you, my companion, my colleague and close friend.
> We had intimate talks with each other and worshiped together in the Temple.
>
> Psalm 55:12–14, TEV

> Be merciful to me, O God, be merciful, because I come to you for safety. In the shadow of your wings I find protection until the raging storms are over.
> I call to God, the Most High, to God, who supplies my every need.
> He will answer from heaven and save me; he will defeat my oppressors. God will show me his constant love and faithfulness.
>
> Psalm 57:1–3, TEV

8

Jealousy
Mom Has a New Boyfriend
Dad Has a New Wife

> There's a green-eyed monster breathing fire
> And the only way to slay him
> Is with a splashing dash
> Of good sense and self-respect.

Just when you and your dad were getting to know each other and have some pretty good times together, someone else has moved into the picture. And he is obviously enjoying himself so much more with her than with you that, again, you feel left out, unloved, and rejected. Be fair, now. You cannot be a spouse to your father, and he has not stopped loving you and being your father just because he has a new wife.

You may be feeling protective toward your mother and resentful of this new woman who appears to be taking her place in your father's life. But, remember, your mom has not had a place in your dad's life for some time.

Stepmothers Are Not All Bad

Not all "wicked stepmother" stories are fairy tales, but most of them are. Chances are, this stepmother of yours is a very nice person, or else your father would not have married her. You may already like her a lot. But it is likely that she is very different from your mother and has different ways of doing things. With some resentment still rolling around inside, you cannot quite bring yourself to accept this person as a relative. The very least you can do in that circumstance is to have some respect for your father and his wife and treat her as politely as possible. No one, not even your new stepmother, expects you to be wildly happy about having her around, at least in the beginning. But there is no excuse for a person who is well on the way to being an adult (that's you) to be rude and act like a spoiled brat. A little kindness can go a long way in this situation. Remember that she is probably feeling pretty anxious, too. It is just possible that you two could wind up liking each other as friends.

Get Any New Rules Clarified

Stepmothers usually have some pretty definite ideas and will even make some rules about kitchen details, mealtimes, and housework. It might be a good idea to sit down with this new female parent to find out what her rules and ideas are. Going over the ground rules can prevent a lot of hard feelings later. No need to be punished for breaking a rule you did not even know existed.

You may be feeling that your space has been invaded—and the least she could do is ask you how things used to be! That probably will not happen, and even if it does, things will never again run the same as they did before. But hold your tongue. This new lady may have some good ideas. Keep an open mind about them, and give her a fair chance! Of course, you can make suggestions from time to time. Try to remember to keep your mom out of them. It is wiser to say, "It works better for me to . . ." than, "My mother always did it this way. . . ."

Contrary to popular opinion, the sole purpose of a stepmother is not to make you unhappy. It is to make your father happy. Even if you think she is going about it all wrong—Keep Out! She is his wife and it is their marriage. Save your ideas about how to please a spouse for your own marriage. If you sense that your father is unhappy, don't be too quick to blame your stepmother. Step back and take a look at the whole scene. He may be unhappy about the tension between his wife and you, since he loves *both* of you.

You will not have to live with your stepmother forever. In a few years you will be an adult and off on your own. The more accepting of his new mate you can be, the easier it will be for Dad to get on with all of the adjustments necessary in a new marriage. Lay the paving stones for warm, welcomed visits to Dad's house in the future by showing respect to his wife now.

Kay

"The big problem is jealousy," said Kay. "She's jealous of me and I'm jealous of her. She's got my dad all the time. Even when he comes to pick us up or takes us home, she's with him."

I encouraged Kay, as I would any young person who feels this way, to try to talk to her stepmother. She may feel that her new stepchild is trying to take over her husband and making unnecessary demands on his time. A talk between the two of you might help to clear the air. Say something like, "I need to have some time alone with my dad, too. I know you have times alone with him and I think that's great, but sometimes it's hard to talk in front of a third person. I don't mean I want you to clear out every time I'm here. I just mean a few minutes every once in a while." My guess is she will be quite understanding, especially if you do not try to monopolize his time.

What If You Are Attracted to Your Father's Wife?

If you are an adolescent boy and Dad has married an attractive woman somewhat younger than himself, you may find yourself in a very awkward situation. She may look good to you, too. In fact, you may be entertaining fantasies of both of you together, without Dad.

It is a little scary to be having thoughts like that about someone who is supposed to be your "mother." Boys do not usually have to deal with those attractions toward their own mothers. But the taboo against sexual interaction is not as strong with stepparents, so keep your romantic dreams in proper perspective and find a girlfriend in your own age group.

Adolescent girls may also need to practice increased modesty. If a stepfather is made acutely aware of your developing figure and increasing attractiveness, he may be tempted to respond in a rather unfatherly way. Take care that the way you dress and act around the house will not be misinterpreted by him.

As a teenager, you are becoming increasingly aware of your sexuality. The average teenager who is struggling to make peace with his or her own emerging sexuality does not think of parents as sexual beings with the same kinds of needs and desires.

You need to be sensitive to what behaviors of yours are provocative or may be interpreted as such by others. Save the flirting for your peers and try to relate to both your parents and stepparents in a straightforward manner.

Mom's Boyfriend

Mom has a boyfriend, and that sense of betrayal is back again. This time you are feeling bad for Dad. No need for that. He is out of the picture (Mom's picture), but she still needs someone, and we have established that is should not be just you. Both of you have needs for relationships with people your own age, both male and female. Most kids are out of the house and on their own by the age of eighteen to twenty-two. What happens to Mom then? If you don't want to stick around and play checkers with her—not at all a healthy idea—then cheer her on to a new mate. It will be much easier for you to make the normal move away from home when the time comes if you do not have any tugs of responsibility for an unmarried parent.

Stepfamilies

Since it is probable that at least one of your parents will remarry, it is also possible that the new stepparent will have children. These children will be your stepbrothers and stepsisters. In some ways a stepfamily is like a diamond. The more faces there are, the more exciting and beautiful it is. But, also like a diamond, the more faces there are, the more points there are to cause irritation, frustration, and tension.

You will probably find those new faces somewhat less than beautiful, at least at first. Kids in this situation approach stepbrothers and sisters with a variety of feelings, ranging from a certain suspicious coolness to a mad infatuation with a new sibling of the opposite sex. It takes time to get to know any person well enough to decide whether or not you like him or her. And being forced into a new family relationship will not hurry that process.

In fact, it may take even longer to learn to like people you see daily. All of their shortcomings will be more than obvious to you, especially if one or more of you are experiencing insecurity and jealousy, magnifying traditional sibling rivalry. You may feel a great deal of resentment toward the newcomer, who is probably equally resentful of you.

Maybe you are forced to share a room with one of these strangers. Since none of us takes kindly to an infringement on our privacy, such a situation will call for some real understanding. A discussion of needs and preferences is called for, and the sooner the better. The best time for this conversation is before either of you has a chance to really get under the other's skin. Try to work out your differences without always calling on your respective parents to take sides.

Would You Believe They're Going to Have a Baby?

Stepbrothers and sisters are one thing—but this one will be a *half*-brother or -sister and you will have to share your parent's time, attention, and affection with one more person. That's not fair! Everybody knows babies are cute and adorable. How can a teenager who cannot control his feet or his voice—or her hair or her zits—compete with a cutesy baby?

Both Gina and Shirley responded in a warm and maternal way to the new family addition. They were willing and eager to be caregivers to the babies. Both report feeling great love and warmth and pride in the new sibling.

Sara

So distressed was Sara by the arrival of a new baby that she was physically abusive of the infant and destructive to clothing of a younger sibling. Of course, these are extremes of the feelings you may experience, and you may find yourself feeling one way one day and swinging the other way the next. That is normal. If you should recognize your negative feelings as being predominant or find yourself taking aggressive action because of them, as Sara did, you should seek help. Seek out that trusted person and talk, talk, talk.

Are You Feeling Like a Misfit?

All of these disruptions in your life have come about without any real input from you. You did not choose divorce, and you had little say in the selection of a stepfamily. You could be feeling pretty left out and without much control. Just when you feel as if you need more control over what happens in your life, it seems that you have less.

Besides all that, you do not really seem to belong in either family. There are new stepbrothers and sisters and you do not look like any of them or share the mutual childhood memories. You may have lost your role as the oldest, the youngest, or the only boy or girl. Maybe you feel like the lonely little petunia in the onion patch. And all those onions can surely bring tears to the eyes. Being separated physically from one parent by divorce and now losing the other one to a new spouse can leave you feeling like a real orphan.

However, there are other faces that come with the remarriage of parents—new aunts, uncles, cousins, and grandparents. Out of all these new people there are bound to be some you like and who respond to you with warmth. Look for them, and enjoy the adventure of getting to know them all.

What Happened to Grandma?

There may be another source of distress after the remarriage of a custodial parent. If, while your parent was single, you lived with or spent extra time with your grandparent(s), you may now be experiencing another loss: the separation from their company. While your parent is busy getting settled into a new marriage, there may not be time for those pleasant trips to Grandma's house.

You may have to blow the dust from that Christmas notepaper and polish up your writing skills. Your grandparents will be feeling lonely, too, and will surely enjoy hearing about your activities, and even how much you miss them. Writing is also a good way to keep in touch with your absent parent. Remember to make your communication a chance to share the good things in your life, as well as the unpleasant details. Don't make your letter a litany of complaints. Phone calls are helpful, especially if there is no hassle about long-distance bills. Be sure there is an understanding about who pays for how many calls and about how long the calls may be. Stay alert to the sensitivity of your stepparent to the contacts you have with your natural parent or grandparents. There is no sense in creating unnecessary unpleasantness.

When David was deeply troubled he wrote Psalm 77. It may help you to read the whole Psalm, since only part of it is printed below:

> I cry aloud to God; I cry aloud, and he hears me.
> In times of trouble I pray to the Lord; all night long I lift my hands in prayer, but I cannot find comfort. . . .
> He keeps me awake all night; I am so worried that I cannot speak.
> I think of days gone by and remember years of long ago.
> I spend the night in deep thought; I meditate, and this is what I ask myself:
> "Will the Lord always reject us? Will he never again be pleased with us?
> "Has he stopped loving us? Does his promise no longer stand?" . . . .
> I will remember your great deeds, Lord; I will recall the wonders you did in the past.
>
> Psalm 77:1–2,4,5–8,11, TEV

9

Living
Let's Get On with It

> The Lord says, "Come,
> I am the rock of your salvation.
> In me is your strength.
> Follow my ways
> And find new life."

What effect will your parents' divorce have on the rest of your life? That is entirely up to you. Some characteristics you received from your parents are unchangeable, such as the color of your eyes, the freckles on your nose, and the size of your feet. But your happiness is entirely your own responsibility. What your parents have done or continue to do will impact on your life only to the extent that you allow.

When God gave us freedom of choice—remember that Adam and Eve story—He gave us the freedom to make decisions that drastically affect our lives. Many things will happen to you over which you have no control, such as your parents' divorce. But you are free to choose how to react to these events.

Adapting to New Expectations

Some kids are better prepared at being adaptable because they have had more experience at coping with unusual events. Some have also had a remarkably good role model.

Lori

Both experience and a positive role model helped Lori adjust to her parents' divorce. She explained: "Not having my dad around wasn't too much more difficult for us, because he was always a traveling salesman of some sort. The fact that we had more responsibilities when he left wasn't more difficult either, because my mother had multiple sclerosis. We had been doing things like the cooking and cleaning and ironing and what not. I took care of my little sister who is eight years younger than I am since she was a baby, so those things weren't the major hassles.

"It helped, too, that we were raised in a very resilient environment. My mom said, 'Look, this is the situation. I can't walk. So, what are we going to do about it? We can cry about it or laugh about it.' So we went to the laughing and working through the situation."

While that background did not make adjusting to and accepting her parents' divorce a "piece of cake," it did help Lori to keep it in a good perspective.

Effects of Divorce on Kids

M. E. Lamb did a study on the effects of divorce on children's personality development. The results were published in 1977 in the *Journal of Divorce*. This study revealed two important findings. The first is that children of divorced parents, compared with children of intact families, are "at risk" for psychological damage. That means with all of the hurts, guilt, and anger related to the divorce, you can get pretty bent out of shape. It does not mean you *have* to. You can be like Lori's mom and say, "This is the situation. We can laugh or we can cry." And you can find people to talk to—people who will help you sort out your feelings and find words to express them.

The second conclusion of Lamb's study was that it is not possible to generalize flatly about "the effects of divorce," because there are no specific consequences that can be identified as the inevitable result of divorce and family breakup.

Divorce can even be beneficial to some children, inasmuch as it signals the end of hostilities, uncertainties, and harmful hatefulness. "Beneficial" does not necessarily mean that the situation is welcome.

Gina

"I was a young child at the time of the divorce and my mother's remarriage," Gina recalls. "I remember that I loved my stepfather dearly. He was so good to us. But I can always remember wishing my mom and dad would get back together again and that my stepparents would marry each other. I remember thinking that because they had divorced before, maybe this would happen again. I don't know why I thought that. There was no logical reason for wanting it. My father had abused Mom and us kids. I knew my mom was happy, and we were happy with my stepfather. No problems. But there was just this biological need to be a 'whole' family."

How Will Your Parents' Divorce Affect Your Own Marriage?

No matter how unpleasant or how amiable a divorce of the biological parents may have been, one of the most permanent scars on a teenager's mind may be the question: "What about my marriage?"

Lori

Reflecting about her parents' divorce, Lori said: "It doesn't debilitate me, but sometimes it holds me back from being a total person. I especially want to know if I'll ever be able to relate successfully with a man, because there's a part of me that's been very hurt. And it takes a long time for me to trust any man."

Chris

"I saw a rotten model so that scares me," added Chris. "Because I saw my parents mess up royally, how do I know I won't do the same thing? Because I've seen that, I'm going to work twice as hard to see that it won't happen. I have fears that if I get married, it will break down like my folks' marriage did. But I believe it will be okay if I work at it—and I mean really work, because I think when marriages break down it's not because they have a year or two of fighting. It's because there were problems since the very beginning. And the answer is not just, 'Ha, ha, we'll sit down and pray around the table and everything is going to be fine.' That doesn't work. If you work at it from the start and really work, then sure, maybe it can be forever. I don't want to walk down the aisle with reservations, thinking in the back of my mind that maybe down the road twenty or twenty-five years from now this guy is going to skip out on me. I don't want to do that. I want to walk down there thinking, 'I'm giving you my life for the rest of my life,' and I want to be assured that it's okay for me. And I want to have enough trust in the person that I do that with to say, 'I trust you completely and I know that what you're saying to me now really matters.'"

Avoiding Marriage Is Probably Not the Answer

You could be saying, "Marriage wasn't such a hot idea for my folks, so maybe I'll just skip that." That would be a sure way to keep from getting hurt. It would also just as surely keep you from experiencing the joy and happiness of a truly loving relationship. Don't be frightened off by your parents' mistakes. Learn from them.

Marie

It has been eight years since Marie's parents' divorce, and she says: "I'm seriously thinking of getting married in the not too distant future. When I was in my senior year of college I was very close to somebody and he asked me to marry him. Back then I used the excuse, 'I have to finish my college education.' But I was really saying, 'I'm too scared to get married. If I get married, we're going to get divorced.' What a dumb thing to say! Just because my parents got a divorce doesn't mean my marriage wouldn't work. The situation that caused their divorce was rather unusual. And yet part of my hesitation at that time was that I just wasn't old enough to get married and I realize that. But another part of it was that I was frightened of having to deal with the possibility of divorce. Now that I'm again considering marriage, it causes me to wonder what will happen.

"If my parents hadn't gotten a divorce, I'd have gone into marriage thinking, 'This is it—until death do us part.' I still do believe that marriage is a very important thing and that you should try as hard as you can to make a go of it, and really try until you have no energy left. But I also realize now—and I'm comfortable in the knowledge—that you *can* get a divorce. I've seen a divorce. I've worked through it with my parents. I've realized that if I get a divorce, life will go on. I still have my career. That doesn't get taken away from me. If I have kids and I get a divorce, I have a career that will enable me to support them.

"I'm entering into marriage a little bit more realistically, I think, than I would have earlier. I realize that there may be mental illness, chronic disability, or financial problems. There are all kinds of problems that can crop up in a marriage. But I think I'm just a lot more realistic about it.

"Sometimes I think it's healthy that I'm considering the option of divorce. This is such a crazy thing to talk about! But it's a realistic thing. You have to think about what kinds of things are going to make you get divorced. And you have to discuss it with the person you're going to marry. What kinds of things are you not willing to deal with? What kinds of things are you going to ask to get out of? If I become chronically ill, is that going to be the end for my husband? Are financial problems going to be the thing I can't handle? Abuse? Alcoholism? Criminal behavior? What codes do we live by? I want to know now, not after we get married. So I talk about those kinds of things with my boyfriend. I think I never would have before. I think people don't talk about those things because they hope they're never going to happen. Realistically, things like that do happen.

"I will mean it when I say, 'Until death do us part.' I would really like that to be true. But you have to face up to the fact that maybe you will not be able to deal with certain stresses in marriage."

You Can Be a Survivor

You do not have to accept that divorce is the fate of most marriages. Good marriages can and do exist for young people whose parents were divorced. But strong, loving marriages never just happen by chance. They are carefully considered and planned. Building a good marriage is somewhat like preparing an elegant banquet. You shop carefully for the partner with the right ingredients for your taste. Measure the amount of humor, industriousness, economic sense, warmth, need for family, career-mindedness, and spiritual life you desire—and choose accordingly. Now begin blending the qualities that each of you bring, seasoning liberally with tolerance and understanding. When occasionally something comes to a boil, remove from the heat and stir in a liberal portion of conversation and good sense.

Include a large measure of spiritual food, and garnish frequently with fun and merriment. Serve with love, which will turn even the lowliest crockery into fine china. Savor the riches of a delightful marriage. Rinse your palate between each course with prayer.

There are many excellent marriage manuals available. You will find a listing of several at the end of this chapter or you might ask your pastor to recommend one or two. Read and discuss together your hopes and dreams for your marriage, anticipating any differences that might cause friction. Seek good counseling before the wedding, and later whenever a problem arises that seems bigger than the two of you can handle.

Do not be crippled by the fear of failure. Open yourself to love and to being loved. Turn often for guidance to the Author of Love:

> . . . .God is love, and whoever lives in love lives in union with God and God lives in union with him.
>
> 1 John 4:16, TEV

> We love because God first loved us.
>
> 1 John 4:19, TEV

> Love must be completely sincere. Hate what is evil, hold on to what is good. Love one another warmly as Christian brothers, and be eager to show respect for one another. Work hard and do not be lazy. Serve the Lord with a heart full of devotion. Let your hope keep you joyful, be patient in your troubles, and pray at all times.
>
> Romans 12:9–12, TEV

> Love is patient and kind; it is not jealous or conceited or proud; love is not ill-mannered or selfish or irritable; love does not keep a record of wrongs; love is not happy with evil, but is happy with the truth. Love never gives up; and its faith, hope, and patience never fail. Love is eternal.
>
> 1 Corinthians 13:4–8a, TEV

Suggested Reading

Andelin, Aubrey P. 1982. *Man of Steel and Velvet*. Santa Barbara: Pacific Press.

Dobson, James. 1975. *What Wives Wish Their Husbands Knew About Women*. Wheaton: Tyndale.

LaHaye, Tim and LaHaye, Beverly. 1976. *The Act of Marriage*. Grand Rapids: Zondervan.

Osborne, Cecil. 1976. *The Art of Understanding Your Mate*. Grand Rapids: Zondervan.

Powell, John. 1974. *The Secret of Staying in Love*. Allen, Texas: Argus Communication.

Shedd, Charlie. 1966. *Letters to Karen*. Nashville: Abingdon.

———. 1968. *Letters to Philip*. New York: Doubleday.